When 10-year-old Ben Tennyson stumbles upon a mysterious alien device in the woods one summer, little does he realise that his life is set to change – forever.

As soon as the watch-like Omnitrix quite literally gets a grip on him, Ben discovers it gives him the ability to transform into 10 different alien super-beings, each one with awesome powers!

Using the Omnitrix to cause super-powered mischief turns out to be fun, but will Ben learn to use his might to fight for good?

READ ON AND FIND OUT . . .

EGMONT

We bring stories to life

Published in Great Britain 2009
by Egmont UK Limited
239 Kensington High Street, London W8 6SA

Ben 10 and all related characters and elements
are trademarks of and © Cartoon Network.
(s08)

Adapted from the animated series by
Glenn Dakin

1 3 5 7 9 10 8 6 4 2

A CIP catalogue record for this title is available from
the British Library

Printed and bound in Great Britain by the CPI Group

CHAPTER ONE

WHAT A NIGHTMARE

It was the big news story of the day.

'We're live on the scene of a high-speed police pursuit,' the TV reporter announced to shocked viewers across the nation. 'An armoured car full of gold has been stolen and the thieves are now making their getaway.

It is believed the thieves also have a hostage!' he added.

It looked bad. The robbers were driving like madmen; pretty soon there would be a massive pile-up on the highway as traffic scrambled to get out of the way of the chase.

Then it happened. Something unexpected. Something totally cool.

Sharp green crystals sprang right up out of the road and ripped into the tyres of the armoured car. Out of control, it spun into the guard rail at the side of the highway.

The police squad cars pulled up, surrounding the stolen car. A shaven-headed thief in high-tech goggles jumped out, dragging the frightened hostage with him. A second member of the gang appeared, carrying an enormous laser cannon.

ZAP! A blast like forked lightning blew one of the squad cars clean off the ground.

'Wait! What's this?' gasped the excited voice of the news reporter. Behind the armed thief, emerging out of the smoke and dust, an incredible figure appeared: a giant being of ice-green crystal.

The thief whirled round, only to see his laser cannon sliced to pieces by a glinting green claw. The robber turned to run, but was lifted up by a huge, fast-growing crystal that sprouted out of the ground and left him dangling helplessly in the air.

'Yes,' said the thrilled news reporter. 'It looks like we have another alien sighting.'

But this was no alien. It was just a regular, ten-year-old human boy. Benjamin Tennyson. And today Ben had morphed into the awesome form of Diamondhead.

The remaining robber gazed up at the green giant who blocked his way. He formed an instant, very sensible plan: he gave up.

'We don't know where these strange creatures come from, but they seem to be here to help,' the news reporter concluded. Diamondhead grinned. The cops moved in – it was all over.

✖ ✖ ✖

Not everyone watching had enjoyed the show. Far out in space, a pair of evil red eyes had seen everything. Vilgax had followed the whole chase on the wall-sized viewing screens in his space ship.

'The Omnitrix – wasted on pointless heroics!' he growled. A small robot looked up, eager to help.

'Shall I send more drones to get it?'

There was a hiss of steam as the doors of the recovery pod opened and the alien strode out. Vilgax was ready to rumble. This evil being was so tall he almost made a hero like Diamondhead look like a toy action figure. He had the face of a sly space-squid, perched on top of a giant body encased in gleaming armour.

'No,' replied Vilgax. 'I will see to this task myself.'

✖ ✖ ✖

'Ugh!' Ben sat up in the dark, wild-eyed and afraid. He was relieved to realise that he was

safe and sound in The Rust Bucket – the big
motorhome owned by his grandpa, Max.

'Another nightmare, Ben?' asked his
grandfather, swiftly arriving at the side of Ben's
bunk.

'It was that weird alien from my vision,'
Ben said, remembering a previous adventure
when the same creepy face had appeared in
his mind. 'Only this one was bigger, uglier and
scarier,' he added.

Ben's cousin Gwen rolled over in the bunk

below him. Her bright-green eyes flashed with annoyance at being woken up.

'Sure you weren't just looking in a mirror?' she asked. Grandpa Max gave a tired smile.

'It was just a bad dream, son,' he said. 'We can talk about it in the morning.' But Ben was still shaken by his nightmare.

'He looked right at me,' Ben protested, 'and he said, "I'm coming for you now!"'

Grandpa Max froze in his tracks. Then, as calmly as he could, he made straight for the driver's seat.

'Change of plan,' he said grimly. 'We're hitting the road right now.'

Gwen groaned. 'It's three in the morning!'

The huge six-wheeler rumbled into life and swung out on to the deserted highway.

'Best way to beat the traffic,' said Grandpa.

❊ ❊ ❊

The sun was shining down on the plains of South Dakota, and curious bison turned their shaggy heads to watch The Rust Bucket roar through their land. It was half a day later, and the Tennysons were nearing their destination.

'I want to make Mount Rushmore by nightfall,' Grandpa Max explained, to fend off yet another question about his need for speed. Ben was bored. He and Gwen had spent countless hours on the road that summer on their endless camping trip. Now, just watching Grandpa scaring the wildlife with his driving was getting a bit old.

'Let me play a game,' Ben begged, watching Gwen at her laptop computer.

'I would,' Gwen said sweetly, 'but I think this will be a good lesson for you to learn how to entertain yourself.'

Ben looked glum. Then he grinned a fiendish grin. He knew how to entertain himself all right. He checked the dial on his Omnitrix, and clicked it into life.

At exactly that moment, orbiting the Earth, Vilgax stirred in his command chair. His monitor systems had just gone wild.

'The Omnitrix has been activated. Pinpoint its location!'

A holographic map of the Earth spun before Vilgax, until it zeroed in on its target: South Dakota, North America. Vilgax smiled.

'I have you now!'

CHAPTER TWO

DREAM COME TRUE?

*G*wen was puzzled, not to mention annoyed. Her computer had suddenly gone crazy; she couldn't make it do a thing. Now the screen had gone black, suggesting total power failure.

'Hey, what gives?' A green stick-man appeared on the monitor.

'Sorry,' its robotic voice informed her, 'you are a loser.' Gwen looked astonished.

'And you always will be!' giggled Ben, who had invaded the computer as Upgrade, his high-tech alien form.

'Get out of my computer!' shouted Gwen. Her laptop had now sprouted legs, and scuttled away from her like a bug.

'What? I'm just entertaining myself,'
teased Ben. 'Oooh, what's this? A diary?' he
added. Now things were getting interesting!
'"Dear Diary,"' Upgrade read, '"my cousin Ben
is such a –"'

'Doofus!' Gwen exploded. 'Knock it off!'
Grandpa Max turned and snapped at Ben.

'Now is not the time to go alien! Do you
understand?' he shouted. Upgrade oozed sadly
out of the computer.

'I was just fooling around,' the floppy

creature sighed, the pale circle of his face blinking glumly. 'What kind of attention could I attract in here?'

In a flash, Upgrade changed back to Ben.

'Never mind,' muttered Grandpa Max.

Ben and Gwen exchanged puzzled looks. Grandpa really was in a weird mood.

❊ ❊ ❊

Unknown to the crew of The Rust Bucket, Vilgax's gleaming ship was poised, far out in space, directly above them.

'We've lost the Omnitrix signal,' came the report. Vilgax peered down on his robotic second-in-command.

'No matter,' Vilgax replied. 'I've narrowed down its location.' The sinister alien turned his tentacled head to gaze at his monitors. They showed images of Ben in his various forms, rescuing people from every kind of peril.

'I know just how to draw this Earthling out.'

Moments later, a great dark shadow fell across the prairies of South Dakota as Vilgax's ship lowered itself to land. A hatch hissed open and out rolled a huge spiked metal ball. Deadly flying probes – robot drones – buzzed alongside like big angry hornets.

A friendly sign greeted the alien visitors: Welcome to Rapid City. The drones zapped it to bits, while the spiked ball rolled on towards the sleepy city.

Screams filled the air as the alien demolition force struck in the heart of downtown Rapid City. The spiked ball powered through the side of an office block, chewing through its concrete walls as if they were soggy cardboard. The drones darted here and there, their deadly lasers destroying parked cars.

KA-BOOM! The central petrol station went up in a sheet of orange flame, a jet-black cloud mushrooming out across the city.

'What's going on over there?' Ben gaped out of the window of the speeding Rust Bucket at the smoke rising up into the blue sky.

'I'm sure the authorities have the situation well in hand,' remarked Grandpa Max, not seeming at all interested. For once, Ben thought his grandfather had called it wrong.

'Looks like it's hero time!'

He checked out the dial on the Omnitrix, clicking through the selection of forms, until he hit the right one. Grandpa Max shot him an anxious glance.

'Ben, I don't think that's the best idea –'

Too late – Ben had made his mind up. He braced himself to face the surge of power, as his cells morphed like wildfire across his whole body.

'Time to turn up the Heatblast on these guys!' The Rust Bucket door flew open and out shot Heatblast himself, his hands glowing like coals, his head a ball of flame, the round Omnitrix symbol displayed on the chest of his red-and-white costume.

'Hey,' he shouted, 'why don't you pick on someone with real firepower?'

The drones didn't know what hit them. Red-hot fireballs blasted them out of the sky, melted their weapons and left them lying in pools of molten metal. Heatblast was having a ball. It wasn't often he got to let rip like this.

But now the fun part was over. Heatblast realised he had been tricked. Hunting his foes, he had been lured into the centre of a whole swarm of angry drones. They hovered around him silently, ready to strike.

'Oh, man, I didn't mean all at once!' he groaned. The drones moved in closer, their weapons crackling with power as they charged up.

'Why do I get the feeling you were expecting me?' Heatblast wondered out loud. Then he leaped into action – spinning in a circle he fired a scorching blast of flame, melting the drone ships one by one, until they all slumped to the ground in a great ring of bubbling metal.

That was when things turned serious. Heatblast was suddenly pinned to a wall by four metal probes that shot at him out of nowhere, ensnaring him in their beams of power. Heatblast was well and truly trapped! He watched, helpless, as a massive spiked ball rolled towards him.

It rumbled to a halt. A hatch opened. An enormous figure emerged, its heavy feet shattering the sidewalk. Vilgax loomed above Heatblast, his narrow red eyes squinting down at his captive.

'You!' gasped Heatblast. 'You're the alien from my visions!'

'At last we meet,' the monstrous creature snarled. 'The being that has caused me so much trouble.'

CHAPTER THREE

MAKING A STINK

*R*apid City was a smoking inferno. Trapped in the middle was Heatblast, and inside Heatblast was Ben. He knew he was facing the battle of his life.

'Who are you?' Heatblast asked.

'I am Vilgax and I have come for the Omnitrix,' rasped an unearthly voice. Ben

needed to play for time while he figured out a way to escape.

'And, uh, I'm guessing you're not with the good guys,' Heatblast said. He knew action spoke louder than small talk at a time like this so, with a sudden effort, he turned up his body heat, melting the devices holding him and tearing himself free of the wall.

Now it was payback time! Heatblast launched an all-out attack on Vilgax, dealing out blow after blow with his fists of fire. Something made him stop and look up; he was punching the giant alien in the ankle and having absolutely zero effect.

Vilgax grabbed Heatblast viciously, swung him back, then hurled him through five tower blocks. It may have been six – Ben found it hard to keep track of the exact number. Heatblast pulled himself up out of the smoking crater where he had finally wound up, and looked worried.

'OK,' he sighed, 'this guy's really tough.'

There was no let-up with this creep. Vilgax was now bounding across town, straight towards Heatblast, at incredible speed.

'I've got to slow him down,' Heatblast told himself. It was time to use his head. Instead of aiming his firepower straight at the alien, he targeted the road in front of him. It smoked, bubbled and melted into a swamp of sticky black tar.

Vilgax's massive feet got stuck in the molten gloop, causing him to topple over like

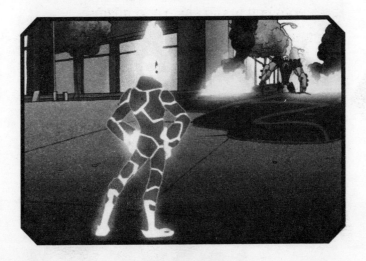

a falling tree. He landed with a satisfying

SHLOCK in the hot goo, and struggled to

escape.

Right then, The Rust Bucket turned up

on the scene. Grandpa Max stared at the fallen

Vilgax in disbelief.

'No!' he gasped. 'It can't be!' He put his

foot down on the accelerator and screeched

towards Heatblast. Gwen threw the door open.

'Grandpa says to get in,' she said. 'Now.'

Heatblast wasn't so sure. He thought he finally had Mr Squid-head where he wanted him.

'I'm just about to kick alien butt!' he protested. **BLEEP!** Heatblast heard the sound he dreaded most. The Omnitrix had decided that playtime was over; in a flash he morphed back into Ben.

The Rust Bucket pulled away – faster than Ben could ever remember it doing before.

'Believe me when I say you do not want to pick a fight with Vilgax,' Grandpa Max said. Ben frowned. One little question sprang to mind.

'Uhhh, how do you know his name is Vilgax?'

Gwen was starting to lose her cool. 'Grandpa, what aren't you telling us?'

Before Grandpa Max could reply, a sudden blast rocked the vehicle from side to side. Gwen whirled round to check the rear view.

'Two robot goons, closing in fast!'

Grandpa Max looked grim. It was time for some serious getaway driving.

'Hold on!' He swerved The Rust Bucket across three lanes of the deserted highway, dodging the energy blasts of the fast-approaching drones.

Again, the deadly craft swooped overhead, but Grandpa Max swung the wheel crazily to shake them off for a second time. He was pleased that he had at least drawn the drones away from other traffic. No more innocent bystanders were going to get caught up in this battle.

BLAM! The enemy was back, its fireballs landing closer than ever. Hurled from side to side of the vehicle, Gwen was clinging on for dear life.

'We can't keep this up forever!' she warned. Grandpa Max stuck to the job. He would keep it up forever if he had to.

'Things are going to get a whole lot

worse if we don't get to Mount Rushmore,' he remarked. Ben was fiddling with the dial of his watch, trying to coax it into giving him another form – fast. Meanwhile, Gwen was close to freaking out.

'Why?' she cried out. 'What's at Mount Rushmore?' Grandpa Max didn't have time to explain.

'You're going to have to trust me,' he said. **THUD!** A sudden impact rocked The Rust Bucket. Something had landed on the roof.

'Well, I'm not going down without a fight!' Ben promised. He'd finally done it. With a grin of delight, he lined up the rings on the watch and a winged figure appeared on the dial. There was a bright glow and there, instead of Ben, was Stinkfly.

'Yes!' The six-legged, four-horned alien bug hovered on its jagged wings and shot out of the door.

'Ben! Wait!' Grandpa Max called.

But Stinkfly wasn't planning on hanging around. For starters, he had to dodge the attacks of those nasty little flying pests. Then he wheeled around in the air, opened his jaws and spewed out a great spinning glob of stink-slime. **POW!** It exploded, taking down a pair of drones with it.

But one of his pursuers had escaped the blast. Stinkfly latched on to the back of the final drone and sliced through its rear section with his diamond-shaped tail. The drone plunged to the ground and exploded in a cloud of smoke. Stinkfly circled the scene of his triumph with glee.

'Floats like a butterfly, stings like a Stinkfly!' he boasted in a voice like the whine of a mosquito. But he hadn't spotted the weird cocoon beneath him. Stinkfly had just flown back over the place where he had just left Vilgax.

The gigantic alien, revived and ready for

action after his spell in the cocoon, ripped his
way out of his glowing red shell, sprang up
and grabbed on to one of Stinkfly's many legs.

'Give me the Omnitrix!' demanded Vilgax.
Stinkfly swooped and soared but his enemy
clung on tight.

'Who is this guy?' Stinkfly wondered
aloud. He summoned up a massive ooze-attack
and squirted Vilgax with a flood of the vilest

goo he had. The big alien was forced to let go and crashed to the ground.

The Rust Bucket, no longer under attack, came to a halt. The dust from Vilgax's fall was starting to clear, and Grandpa Max could finally study the scene and assess the situation. He suddenly put his foot hard down on the accelerator and sped away from the action.

'Where are we going?' asked Gwen in surprise, now seated up front with Grandpa Max. 'We have to help Ben!'

'We will,' said Grandpa Max at the wheel. 'But first we'll need to get some special help.'

'Let me guess – at Mount Rushmore,' Gwen suggested. Grandpa Max said nothing, but drove on like a man with a mission.

'Grandpa, you're really freaking me out,' Gwen added. She had never seen her grandfather like this before, and she realised they were probably facing their biggest crisis yet.

CHAPTER FOUR

CAUGHT IN A TRAP

*G*randpa Max and Gwen had left the scene of Vilgax's fall just in time. The evil alien, now fully recovered, had climbed back to his feet and was madder than ever. He stomped off in pursuit of his prey. Vilgax couldn't fly, but he bounded across the city, from rooftop to rooftop, leaving a trail of crushed office blocks behind him, like broken sandcastles.

Stinkfly hovered on the edge of the city, away from any high buildings, but he still he wasn't safe. With a final incredible bound, Vilgax snatched him out of the sky. Stinkfly was like a little bug in the alien's huge claw. As far as Vilgax was concerned, it was game over.

'I grow tired of this,' he muttered, and, showing surprising skill for a towering alien menace, he lightly touched the centre of the Omnitrix with the tip of his horny claw. There was a **BLEEP!** and suddenly Ben was hanging there helpless.

'Hey, how'd you do that?' Ben complained. Vilgax gazed at the ten-year-old Earth boy with surprise, fury and disgust.

'A child?' he roared. 'The Omnitrix is in

the hands of a mere child?'

Vilgax tried to remove the device, but it unleashed a massive shock, blasting the alien head-over-tentacles into a wall. Ben tried to scuttle away and lose himself in the rubble, but his enemy had grabbed him again in seconds.

'It appears the Omnitrix has already merged with your own DNA,' Vilgax said.

'I, uh, don't suppose that means you're going to let me go, does it?' Ben asked hopefully.

'Hardly,' came the cold reply. Vilgax's landing craft, the great spiked ball, rolled up. The alien tossed Ben inside, then climbed in after him. The door slammed shut, and the ball rumbled away.

�֎ ✖ ✖

Rising up from the plains of South Dakota, Mount Rushmore loomed before them. The great stone faces of four presidents, carved into the mighty rock, gazed down as The Rust Bucket roared up the winding track into the heart of the hills. Gwen glanced around, nervous.

'I don't think tourists are allowed on this road,' she said. Grandpa shook his head with a knowing smile.

'We're not tourists,' he said. 'We're tenants.' He brought The Rust Bucket to a stop at a remote spot next to a sign saying 'road closed'. Then he hit a secret switch under the dashboard.

There was a grinding noise, a sudden jolt, then the sound of powerful machinery whirring into life. A large circular platform appeared under the vehicle and lowered it down into a hidden shaft.

Grandpa Max and Gwen were in a cavernous underground bunker, a secret base located behind the faces of those famous presidents of old. The whole place was deserted, as if abandoned many years ago. Gwen looked around with awe. She was gazing at row upon row of secret compartments. Grandpa Max, totally at home in this incredible place, pulled open one of the oversized drawers.

Inside was a weird device. Weird as in amazing – amazing as in seriously cool futuristic technology. Gwen had finally had enough.

'That's it!' she shouted, folding her arms. 'I'm not taking another step until you tell me what's going on!'

Grandpa Max swung round, holding the

biggest gun Gwen had ever seen in her life – and that included stuff she'd seen in movies. To operate the weapon, Grandpa Max was kitted up in a special visor. He pressed a switch to charge up the gun and blue energy crackled to life in a see-through tube.

'I wasn't exactly your normal plumber when I retired,' he said.

✹ ✹ ✹

Ben was sure he must have been in tighter spots than this – but right now he couldn't quite remember any. He was trapped in the control room of Vilgax's spaceship, his left arm – the one attached to the Omnitrix – was swallowed up inside a gigantic clamp. His other limbs were held in beams of energy. On top of this, he was suspended high above the ground so that Vilgax could get a better look at him.

'A child,' Vilgax murmured, with hatred in his voice. 'I should've suspected as much.' Gigantic screens revealed every detail of Ben's biology, his DNA, the type, size and number of his every molecule. Another set of laser projections revealed the forms he had morphed into, including XLR8, the tiny alien Grey Matter and Four Arms.

'The Omnitrix being used as a plaything!' Vilgax snorted.

'Hey, I've saved a lot of people by going

hero!' Ben protested. The giant alien ignored
him.

'You hold the key to a power struggle
so ancient, so vast, it is beyond your
comprehension,' Vilgax said. A holographic
image appeared before Ben's eyes, as if it were
beamed directly from the alien's mind, showing
a terrible cosmic war; an incredible army
defeating all before it. And every soldier in that
army was a different one of Ben's forms. XLR8,
Heatblast, Stinkfly, side by side in a ruthless
attacking force.

'Picture an entire army,' Vilgax said,
'each in command of an Omnitrix – and all at
my command! I will be invincible! I will rule
the universe!'

Ben didn't like what he was seeing. He
struggled helplessly against the weird device
that held him aloft.

'And the only thing between me and my
destiny is you,' Vilgax growled. Then a bank of

instruments rose up through the floor, bristling
with probes, drills and an endless variety of
gleaming blades.

CHAPTER FIVE

MAX ATTACK

The Rust Bucket was back on the road.
Grandpa Max was now tearing back towards
the scene of the action as fast as he had left it
minutes before. Except now Grandpa believed
he had the tools to do the job.

'This weapon,' he said, glancing at the
outsized cannon he had removed from the secret
base, 'is keyed into Vilgax's bio-signature.
Hopefully, it'll take him down for good this time.'
Gwen took a moment to let this sink in.

'This time?' she asked. Grandpa Max's
eyes stayed on the road, which was being
gobbled up at an incredible rate by the
speeding motorhome.

'There's a small red button under that cabinet,' he told Gwen. 'Press it.'

Gwen did so. A secret compartment flipped open in the dashboard, revealing a high-tech, laser-display tracking system. To Gwen's increasing surprise, there was already a red dot bleeping on the map – revealing the location of Ben and the Omnitrix.

'GPS-assisted tracking system,' Grandpa Max said. 'It's locked on the watch's signal. You navigate.'

❉ ❉ ❉

Back on the spaceship, Vilgax had selected the fiendish alien probe he wanted to use on his annoying human foe first. He chose a blade that looked to Ben like an outer-space tin-opener. The robotic servants bustled about checking the status of the ship's weapon systems. Countless tiny drones made the ship ready for departure.

'Prepare for take off!' Vilgax announced.

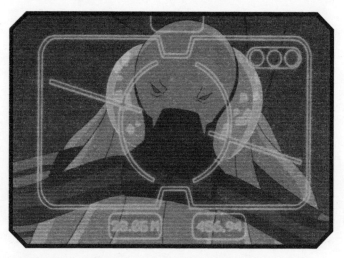

'Once we're in orbit, I will finally have the pleasure of destroying this miserable planet once and for all.' Vilgax raised his shimmering blade. Ben stared with terror.

'I'm going to enjoy this,' smiled Vilgax. The floor was shaking. The great spaceship was powering up its engines ready for lift off.

✹ ✹ ✹

Gwen had always thought it would be kind of cool to go off-road in The Rust Bucket, but not quite like this. Grandpa Max, his jaw set in grim determination, was speeding downhill straight towards the alien craft. Gwen couldn't bear to look. Was he just going to crash right into it?

'We have to get aboard!' Grandpa Max said.

'Get aboard?' gasped Gwen. 'How?' Her grandfather grinned cheekily and, for a split second, Gwen was reminded of her cousin Ben's face when he was cooking up a surprise for her. Grandpa, it turned out, had another secret panel hidden away in his dashboard.

A massive, high-tech battering ram sprang from the front of The Rust Bucket. Gwen squeezed her eyes shut as they hit the side of the spaceship at full speed.

KA-BOOM! The impact shook the whole ship. Grandpa Max blasted the horn to announce his arrival. The Rust Bucket smashed through the outer hull, straight into the control centre, slamming right into Vilgax. The force of the crash carried the alien across the room and buried his body deep into the far wall.

'Warning! Hull breach! Power surge!' the robot drones reported, rushing about like headless chickens. It was too late to stop the vast ship from taking off, and it lurched into the sky, out of control.

The power surge in the command centre had lit up the Omnitrix. Sparks flashed in the air around Ben's wrist. Ben wriggled, desperately trying to escape from his bonds. Vilgax was back on his feet and bearing down on him again, determined to cut the precious device free.

'Claws off my grandson, Vilgax!' Grandpa Max appeared through the smoke, aiming his special weapon right at the alien.

'Grandpa!' Ben could hardly believe his eyes. Grandpa Max had suddenly, amazingly, turned into an all-action hero. Was it a dream?

'Tennyson!' Vilgax hissed, with a trace

of grudging respect. It was clear the two had history.

Right now, Grandpa Max had just one thing on his mind – bringing down the monster that dared to threaten his family.

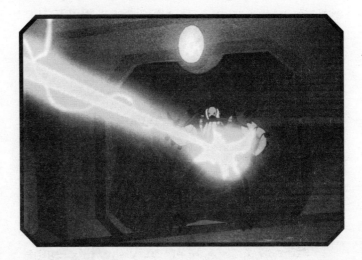

BLAM! A streak of blue lightning blasted Vilgax straight through the wall of his control room. He crashed out of sight in a cloud of smoke. Ben could only stare, open-mouthed, at this new version of Grandpa Max – the alien-butt kicker!

'You know this guy?'

'It's a long story,' Grandpa Max replied. But before he could say any more, the Omnitrix started to go haywire. It pulsed with power, sending Ben through a crazy series of transformations: first the lean, mean XLR8, then the sparkling Diamondhead, followed by a drooling Wildmutt, and then Four Arms.

'Hey, what's going on?' Ben cried out.

'The power surge must have affected the watch!' Grandpa said. Ben was not complaining. As Four Arms, he finally had the power to wrench himself free from his bonds and trash Vilgax's nasty device. It was payback time.

The whole spaceship was now in a state of high alert. Just as Gwen emerged from The Rust Bucket, a swarm of flying drones zoomed into the control room, blasting everything in sight. They were determined to zap the intruders even if they had to wreck their own ship to do it.

'Look out!' shouted Gwen. Four Arms didn't need to be told – he had the power to reach out and swat these little pests like mosquitoes. He raised a mighty pair of fists; he was going to enjoy this!

BLEEP! The Omnitrix flashed and Four Arms morphed into the phantom form of Ghostfreak. Now his grey, ectoplasmic fists flew straight through the drones, with all the impact of a light summer breeze.

'Oh, man!' groaned Ghostfreak in his creepy voice. The drones slipped through his spooky body and continued their rampage. Another explosion shook the ship – the power surge was causing a system overload on a massive scale. Vilgax's battleship had never faced such a crisis before.

Before Ben could figure out his tactics as Ghostfreak, the alien ghoul morphed into the tiny, bug-eyed form of Grey Matter. The drones circled round for another wave of attack.

Grey Matter leaped on-board a passing drone, creeping into its workings. He used his incredible alien brain to make a few smart changes to the programming. **KA-BOOM!** As Grey Matter jumped to safety, the device self-destructed, showering metal fragments on all sides.

'A little alien know-how, and the toaster is toast,' Grey Matter smiled to himself. But the mini genius didn't hang around for long. **BLEEP!** Now Ben had morphed into Upgrade. Gwen, caught in the middle of all the action, was trying to take cover – but she was directly in the drones' line of fire. Ben had to do something quickly, or his cousin could soon be history!

Like a big black jellyfish, Upgrade slurped into the workings of the next drone that passed by. This one was the daddy of them all. Upgrade invaded the drone's systems, changed its core program and morphed it into a gigantic floating buzzsaw. It spun round crazily, cutting up every other drone that came its way.

'Try picking on someone your own size!' Upgrade said. Grandpa Max was getting in on the action too, using his giant laser cannon to take out more of the robots. Against all the odds, it actually looked as if the Tennysons were winning this battle.

KA-BOOM! A power surge blew another hole in the side of the hull. The room tilted. The spaceship gave a sickening lurch, then went into a nosedive – down towards the Earth. Grandpa Max's face told Gwen how dire their peril had become.

'I've got to get the ship under control!' Grandpa Max said. He raced over to the nearest monitor station, studying the screens and read-outs like an experienced astronaut.

Nobody had noticed a huge, dark shape rising up out of the smoke in the smashed-up control room.

'He can fly a spaceship?' asked Upgrade, looking at Grandpa Max with bewilderment. Gwen grinned, while taking a drill to a passing robot drone.

'At this point, nothing surprises me!' she replied.

WHAM! Vilgax was back. He smashed Grandpa Max clean across the room, almost through the gaping hole The Rust Bucket had made in the other side.

'Grandpa!' Ben and Gwen cried in one voice. Vilgax stomped Grandpa Max to the ground, holding him down under his armoured boot. Grandpa groped for his fallen laser cannon, but it was out of reach.

'Your weapon won't help, Tennyson.' Vilgax sneered. 'As you can see, I'm much stronger than I was at our last encounter.' The towering alien raised a cruel claw, ready to strike a final blow.

'Nooo!' Upgrade hurled himself at Vilgax,

hit him at full speed and sent them both

tumbling out of the hole in the wall.

'Ben!' Grandpa Max cried.

CHAPTER SIX

OUT WITH A BANG

The stone face of President Abe Lincoln looked on as Vilgax plummeted past him and smashed into the ground. Upgrade was far luckier. He morphed his body until it was as thin as a parachute and was now floating happily on the breeze.

BLEEP! Upgrade suddenly morphed into Ripjaw – a big, heavy amphibian. Ripjaw could definitely not float on a breeze. He crash-landed on President Lincoln's nose with a painful thud.

'Sometimes I hate this watch,' snarled Ripjaw. Using all his strength, the razor-toothed alien hauled his pale-white, scaly body all the way up to the top of the head. There he lay, gasping. Ripjaw had one, fatal weakness.

'Can't breathe,' he panted. 'Need water!'
A dark shadow fell over Ripjaw's helpless form.

'You are a slippery little fish, child. But
no longer.' Vilgax stretched out a claw towards
the Omnitrix – but there was a sudden whoosh.
Ripjaw had vanished.

Vilgax spun round, confused. There,
zooming across the presidential heads behind
him, was XLR8, his sleek body, stripy tail and
black pointy head glinting in the sunshine.

'I can still give you a run for your money!' quipped the speedster. But Vilgax didn't believe anything could get away from him. Bounding with unbelievable speed, he launched himself after Ben.

The alien came to a halt on the head of President Jefferson. He looked from side to side. Impossible – his foe had completely disappeared!

'You can't hide from me forever, boy!' Vilgax roared.

'Wasn't planning on it! Peek-a-boo!' XLR8 called out. There was a cloud of dust, a roar like a tornado, and XLR8 raced towards his enemy at ramming speed. He hit Vilgax with maximum force, bouncing back on impact. Vilgax hardly even registered the attack.

'Urgh,' groaned XLR8. 'I'm gonna feel that tomorrow.'

'For you, there is no tomorrow,' growled Vilgax, bringing down his mighty fist. XLR8

streaked away in the nick of time, and the alien
was pounding dirt again.

'You can't escape me,' Vilgax said,
bearing down on his foe, fists flying. Finally, he
caught hold of XLR8, swinging him round and
hurling him into the rock face. Clouds of dust
filled the air but, when they cleared, XLR8 had
gone, and a being of glistening green crystal
stood before Vilgax.

'Special delivery!' said Diamondhead.
The green hero unleashed a two-fisted attack,
battering Vilgax with his diamond-hard fists,

SMASH SMASH SMASH! The alien hardly
flinched. Diamondhead looked down. That
shattering sound had been his own fists. He
was now battering Vilgax with two broken
stumps.

'Oh, man! I guess I should've seen that
coming,' said Diamondhead. He looked up and
saw his enemy about to pummel him into the
ground. This time there was no escape. As
he braced himself for the blow, Diamondhead
heard a faint **BLEEP**.

WHOOM! Vilgax's fist passed straight
through Ghostfreak and hit nothing but the
ground.

'Yesss!' whooped Ghostfreak, in his
creepy voice. 'Sometimes I love this watch!'
The one-eyed phantom sank into the rock and
passed safely through the other side. At last,
Ben had escaped his relentless attacker.

❈ ❈ ❈

Grandpa Max and Gwen sat side by side in The Rust Bucket, ready for the drive of their lives. The great spaceship had finally hit the earth, ploughing a mighty furrow across the South Dakota plains. Robot drones squawked, panicked and collided on all sides.

'Better hang on to something,' Grandpa Max warned. 'This might get a little bumpy.' He grinned and put his foot down.

Gwen could hardly bear to look. Grandpa activated the battering ram and powered the six-wheeler through the walls of Vilgax's ship, smashing everything in its path. Gwen shut her eyes as they ripped through the hull again and flew towards the green grass of planet Earth.

There was a loud thump and a screech of brakes as The Rust Bucket hit the ground and screamed to a halt. They were out. Behind them, the vast spaceship lay jammed into the ground. Grandpa Max and Gwen sighed. They were both still in one piece, but shaken.

'You all right, Gwen?' Grandpa asked. His granddaughter nodded.

'At times like this, going back to school doesn't seem too bad,' she said. Then they heard heavy footfalls stomping towards the vehicle. Gwen looked round, hopeful.

'Ben?'

❈ ❈ ❈

Ghostfreak slipped through the rocks as only he could. There was smoke and dust everywhere from the crash-landing of the spaceship. Suddenly, he spotted a familiar sight in a deep rut up ahead – The Rust Bucket.

'Grandpa? Gwen?' Ghostfreak phased through the back of the vehicle and searched it. There was no sign of his family. When he emerged through the front of the van, he immediately discovered what had happened to them. Vilgax was standing in front of him,

Grandpa Max in one claw and Gwen in the other.

Ghostfreak morphed into Wildmutt. The big orange alien-hound snarled furiously, its fangs dripping and its powerful hind legs crouched and ready to spring. But he didn't attack. He knew it was hopeless.

'It's your choice – you, or them,' Vilgax said grimly. Wildmutt seethed with anger, then backed away and hung his head. Vilgax tossed

Grandpa Max and Gwen aside, then touched Wildmutt's Omnitrix symbol. The ferocious creature instantly morphed into Ben.

'How noble,' said Vilgax, carrying the helpless figure of Ben towards his crashed ship. The big alien lumbered through a hole in the shattered hull of his vessel. He was astonished to hear a familiar voice shouting after him.

'Vilgax! No! Don't go back in there!' It was Grandpa Max.

'Foolish Earthling,' he sneered, dropping Ben to the floor. 'Why would I –' then his words dried up. He had seen the warning lights flashing inside his ship.

'The auto-destruct sequence has begun!' he hissed in disbelief. A giant metal piston was pounding away in the control room, pumping explosive materials into the ship's power core. The ship lurched into the air.

Vilgax raced to his control console. He tried to turn off the auto-destruct, but his only reward was a massive energy shock. Ben slipped into the shadows and sneaked towards the giant laser cannon that Max had dropped earlier.

'Tennyson! You are the thorn in my side!' Vilgax raved. **ZA-AP!** Suddenly, he was rocked by a colossal laser blast. He crashed to the floor, the massive piston collapsing on top of him. Ben stepped forward, barely able to carry the enormous smoking weapon.

'Guess it runs in the family,' grinned Ben. Vilgax, his strength sapped by the ray,

struggled under the fallen piston, unable to escape.

'Nooooooo!' he roared. The warning lights were still flashing, and the damaged ship careered across the sky. It was now so high that the air pressure was already sucking broken drones through the hole in the hull. Ben morphed into Heatblast and leaped after them.

He made it just in time. **KA-BOOM!** The ship exploded, torn apart in a blinding triple fireball.

Heatblast surfed a streak of fire towards the ground, triumphant. He hit the ground like a comet, ploughing a great smoking trench in the beautiful South Dakota countryside.

Moments later, Gwen and Grandpa Max raced on to the scene, stumbling through the smoke and mud, desperately looking for Heatblast.

The fiery hero was there no more. Perched on a pile of mud, calm as you like, was a happy

ten-year-old boy – Ben. Grandpa Max and Gwen
rushed towards him. Ben turned, his face aglow
with the reflected heat of the great inferno in
the sky.

　　'Not bad for a doofus,' smiled Gwen. Ben
grinned back. Then he gave Grandpa Max a
long, thoughtful look.

　　'Grandpa,' he said. 'We need to talk.'
Grandpa Max gave a knowing smile. When
it came to secrets, he hardly knew where to
begin.